THE VIG

MCGILL AND GROPPER THRILLERS
BOOK FOUR

ANDREW DAVIE

For Thelma

ACKNOWLEDGMENTS

Thank you, Heather, for reading an earlier version and suggesting feedback, Tyler for the edits, and Miika, Petteri, and Next Chapter for giving these characters a new home.

HONG KONG, JUNE 1996

GROPPER WAS ON THE SIDEWALK OUTSIDE OF A ramen shop and across the street from Lloyd's Bar in Tsim Sha Tsui. He covertly watched Kwun in the reflection in the window. Kwun had dyed blonde hair in a pompadour and wore a black leather jacket, the favored look of a rockabilly musician from a bygone era. Kwun closed the door of his car and dragged a comb through his hair. Some women walked by, and Kwun called out to them. Gropper couldn't hear what was said due to the traffic. However, the women paused, answered Kwun, and continued to walk away. One of them looked back over her shoulder. Kwun had a reputation as a ladies' man, and as far as Gropper was concerned, this helped confirm it.

Kwun watched the girls disappear. Afterward, he made his way to the bar. Going to Lloyd's every Friday night had become a ritual. Kwun would have two glasses of wine and review his business transactions from the week.

The bar was heavily fortified, so Kwun never had to worry about anything. Kwun would usually stay for an hour, and then he would head home. Gropper had analyzed the schedule and decided this would be the best place to handle business. It would be difficult, but if Gropper was successful, it would leave everyone in utter confusion, and practically ensure Gropper's escape. Gropper waited another minute after Kwun had gone inside before he crossed the street himself. Inside, the bar was quiet. It was a classy place, postmodern, and dimly lit. Against the right wall were shelves with rows of liquor bottles. The wine cellar was downstairs. Tables for two to four people were scattered throughout the room.

Kwun sat by himself at a table near the back. A notepad and a glass of red wine were the only items visible on his table. Two other patrons sat at various points between the entrance and the back. Each of them worked for the syndicate. One of them was reading a book, and another listened to music and mouthed along with the words. The bartender was the only person in the place who didn't appear to be connected.

Kwun himself would be another story. Even though he was higher up in the organization, and certainly above getting his hands dirty, he enjoyed mixing it up. He was easily enraged, which suited Gropper's plan nicely. Gropper opened the door and strode in as if he was inebriated but trying with all his energy to look completely sober.

"I'm sorry," the bartender began to say to Gropper, "this is a private club."

The bartender made a gesture that suggested Gropper should stop and turn around.

"I just want one drink," Gropper said.

Gropper had already started walking toward the back with the confidence of someone who would be able to talk his way into having a drink, even if this was a private club. Once the bartender realized Gropper wasn't going to listen, the bartender barked a quick command to the muscle.

Both men immediately lifted their heads and stood simultaneously to address the problem. Gropper, however, had already made it to the rear of the establishment. He stumbled a little to give off the proper impression and banged into the corner of Kwun's table. It was enough of a shot to knock the wine glass onto its side and splash the contents on Kwun's notebook.

Immediately, Gropper began to apologize and grabbed at a place setting on a nearby table. The bartender started yelling at the two others who, though they clearly could have destroyed the bartender, took his abuse without comment. They moved quickly to grab the interloper when Kwun put his hand up to stop them.

Kwun finished assessing the damage and looked at Gropper. "Why don't we talk about this?" he asked calmly.

"Thank you; that would be great," Gropper said. He handed a napkin to Kwun, who blotted at his shirt and pants. Gropper took a seat at the table and continued to apologize without stopping for a breath. His words came on in a stream of consciousness barrage. However, almost as soon as Gropper had sat down at the table, Kwun walked toward the rear of the place. Gropper stood, followed, and continued his apology.

"I mean, I'd be happy to buy you another round. Just let me know what you were drinking," Gropper said, and hurried so he could keep up with the man.

Together they snaked through a storage room full of boxes of booze toward a door that led to the back alley. Kwun opened the door and walked outside. Gropper followed.

"Or, if you wanted something else?" Gropper continued to say when they made it outside.

There weren't any cameras. Management had assumed no one would be stupid enough to deface or burglarize their property. So, they had forgone installing any protective measures. Except for tonight's accident, it had been a long time before there had been any trouble at all.

"What are you thinking?" Gropper asked.

Kwun had stopped walking and still looked in the opposite direction. Gropper couldn't see his face.

"Let me see," Kwun said. He turned around quickly and hit Gropper.

Gropper fell to the ground. "Jesus!" Gropper yelled.

Since he was a boy, Kwun had studied and trained in various disciplines, but his instructors had always remarked about his inability to control his temper. It had been the sole reason he'd been disqualified from almost all the tournaments in which he had competed. It was also what had made him such a brutal enforcer.

Kwun grabbed Gropper under the armpits and lifted him. Gropper swayed from side to side. Blood flowed from his nose and upper lip where he had been struck. Then, just as suddenly, he stopped swaying and became rigid. On his way outside, Gropper had swiped a saltshaker from one of the tables and kept it in his palm. He had taken the punch from Kwun and sold it as if his attacker had connected and done some real damage.

When Gropper was certain Kwun had bought it, Gropper gave up the ruse. He positioned the saltshaker so the domed top protruded from between his middle and ring fingers. Gropper delivered a textbook blow. He felt the resistance as the saltshaker pierced Kwun's eye.

Kwun fell to the ground almost immediately, and his body began to spasm. There was no scream or sounds other than Kwun's limbs flailing. Gropper removed the saltshaker from Kwun's ocular cavity and deposited it in a plastic bag he'd had in his pocket. Once it was secure, he walked from the alley to the street corner and then the metro station. He threw the plastic bag with the saltshaker into the trash can.

It was still early enough for crowds to be on the platform, so he blended in with them, and boarded the train when it arrived.

The office was large and decorated in very severe tones of gray. Trophies of the heads of various animals adorned the walls and a large mural rested on the far wall, which depicted some sort of glorious sword battle from hundreds of years previous. The office was a converted apartment in the Mid-Levels of Hong Kong, close to the world's longest escalator.

The desk was massive, more like a conference table. Behind it sat a man who seemed to be engulfed by his chair. His hair was slicked back, and he had an ease about him. However, lurking just beneath the surface, Gropper sensed the man had an enormous capacity for violence.

Behind the man stood another, adorned in a track suit with a split eyebrow. At five-five the man wasn't outwardly intimidating, but he looked like he knew how to handle himself in a physical confrontation. He also didn't exude calmness anywhere close to the man in the chair: Edgar Chen.

Chen may have been fifty or seventy. He was in relatively good shape. He had all his hair, which had remained black without the use of products. Though the capacity for violence never disappeared, Gropper could not get a read on Chen. The man had incredible control.

Chen reached into a desk drawer, removed an envelope and a cigarette from a gold case and lit the tip with a weatherproof lighter. He took a drag and slid the envelope toward Gropper.

Gropper thumbed through the money without taking it from the envelope. Satisfied it was all there, he put it in his jacket pocket. Chen placed his cigarette in an ashtray near a decanter of what Gropper could only imagine was expensive Scotch.

"A drink?" Chen asked.

"Sure, thank you."

Chen produced two glasses from his desk, poured from the decanter, and handed one to Gropper.

"For handling the unpleasantness," Chen said, and they clinked glasses.

Gropper assumed Chen had been referring to Gropper's removal of Kwun, who had been Chen's nephew. It was a complicated situation.

Chen had revealed some of the details: Kwun had committed an irrevocable loss of face. Gropper hadn't pressed for the details. He sipped his drink. It was cognac, and Gropper was certain if he had asked Chen about it, the man would have been able to give him a lesson on everything about it, from its history to processing; Chen seemed like the sort of person who knew the difference between Sevruga and Ossetra caviar.

"I appreciate the offer to continue to work for you, Mr. Chen," Gropper began, "but I'm afraid I won't be able to accept."

While it certainly would have paid well and he would no doubt excel at whatever tasks were put in front of him, it wasn't his line of work. Killing would always be necessary, but he wasn't an assassin. Gropper took another sip of his drink. Chen had not exhibited any change in his appearance; he remained dispassioned.

The muscle behind Chen started speaking rapidly in Cantonese. Gropper didn't know the man's given name, but he was referred to by the moniker Shui Ni, which roughly translated to "cement".

Chen put up his hand and answered Shui Ni. He had remained calm, though his subordinate was clearly agitated. While Gropper didn't know the subject of the conversation, he assumed it had to do with Gropper's refusal to work for Chen being taken as an insult. Not to mention that Shui Ni probably resented the fact an outsider had been brought in to handle the situation with Kwun. He was probably exhibiting his anger at both. Shui Ni's voice rose, and he began to gesture toward Gropper.

Gropper had done his due diligence on Chen and his organization. Shun Ni's reputation as a fighter had preceded him. At one point, the man had trained as a professional fighter and held his own against Sagat 3-K Battery, a notable Thai fighter who'd been a Muay Thai champion before he'd transitioned into boxing. While he had been training, Shui Ni had won thirty-eight out of forty fights by knock out. That was ninety-five percent.

Shui Ni finished his diatribe and took a step forward. At the same time, Gropper stood, grabbed a cylindrical glass paperweight off Chen's desk, and threw it at Shui Ni. The projectile didn't make a sound as it left Gropper's hand, but it made a hollow smack as it struck Shui Ni in the chest. Shui Ni mouthed a yell, clutched his chest, and sank to the floor.

He tried to breathe, which sounded like the detaching of Velcro. Chen simply took a drag of his cigarette. Gropper had begun to close the distance between him and Shun Ni, who had made it onto his knees and was now dovening like he was in prayer.

Gropper eyed Chen to see if the man would call Gropper off, but he simply continued to watch as if he were at a sporting event. Perhaps Chen had anticipated this would happen and was willing to have Shun Ni humiliated so the man would learn some more control.

Shun Ni had stopped rocking. He put his right hand out as if he were looking for something to hold on to, so he might drag himself to his feet. His breathing was still labored but he no longer sounded like a three-pack-a-day smoker. Shun Ni's head bent, so he was not prepared when Gropper took hold of the index and middle fingers of Shui Ni's outstretched hand. Out of the corner of his eye, Gropper checked to see if Chen had reached for a firearm from his desk. Instead, the man had topped off his drink. The gesture seemed to confirm Chen would be fine with whatever Gropper did next.

Shui Ni's eyes lit up as the pain registered in his cortex as Gropper squeezed. Shui Ni didn't make a sound this time. He collapsed, face forward, onto the floor. Gropper had incorporated many different exercises into his workout, including No. 2 Captains of Crush Hand Grippers to build finger strength. That particular gripper required the equivalent of 195 pounds of pressure to close.

The disc jockey went on to describe how the original members of KISS reunited and were playing a tour. One of the groups that would be supporting them was named Alice in Chains and coming up next was Alice's song, "It Ain't Like That."

It was one of the few stations the radio got from the US. Gropper didn't really care for that type of music, but its heavy-chord progression and distortion were exactly what he needed for his workout. He let loose with a five-punch combination and the heavy bag swayed.

The chains creaked and the sound of his fists hitting the material echoed throughout the gym.

No classes were underway. No amateurs strutted around thinking they were anything special; no one bothered him. It was the way he preferred it. The bell rang and Gropper took a swig of water. The bell sounded again and Gropper went back to hitting the bag. He slipped in a patented straight right to the body and heard the familiar smack. When placed correctly, it was a devastating body shot. Circling to the other side of the bag, he threw another combination.

Another round of boxing, and Gropper would switch to a different discipline. He was about to mount another attack on the bag when the music cut off. A man stood by the console and held the stereo power cord in his hand. The man was a foreigner.

"Help you with something?" Gropper walked closer and removed his gloves.

The man looked to be in his early thirties. He wore a suit and had a hundred-dollar haircut. The suit hid the man's physique, but Gropper could tell the man had training by the way he moved.

"Gropper," the man said as a statement rather than a question, which didn't bode well. Before Gropper could make any further assessments of the situation, the man grabbed a pair of tonfas that had been hanging on the wall and charged. Since the gym catered to a wide array of disciplines, littered throughout was equipment for martial arts, boxing, and more.

Tonfas were similar to police issue nightsticks, a piece of cylindrical wood with a perpendicular handle about a third of the way down. This man clearly knew how to use them and opened with a pretty severe move. The man could have easily come into the gym with a firearm but based on his acquisition of weapons, it suggested the man adhered to a code; moreover, he probably wanted to measure his abilities against Gropper's.

Gropper sidestepped the first strike, which would have easily broken his collarbone had it connected, and as the man swung for his second strike, Gropper had already closed the distance between them, and buried his folding knife between the man's ribs.

The men let out a yell. He dropped his weapons, began to hyperventilate, and walked in a circle. He looked like he was going to ask Gropper a question but fell to his knees before he could say anything.

Gropper bent down and checked for a pulse. The man was dead. Thankfully, no one else would be in the gym for another few hours, so it would give him plenty of time to take care of removing the body and cleaning up. While Gropper regretted that he wouldn't be able to find out who'd hired this man, it did mean Gropper was no longer in hiding. This wasn't retribution for Gropper turning down Edgar Chen or what he'd done to Shui Ni.

The man who lay dead on the gym floor had been contracted to kill Gropper from an international client. His time in anonymity was done. It was probably time to head back to the States.

… Perhaps Gropper would give McGill a call.

Gropper had arrived at the lobby of the International Financial Center on Hong Kong Island without a hitch. He had gotten in line for a hot tea at Starbucks. It was packed, so at least ten people milled about in front of him. He still hadn't gotten used to how crowded it could get in the city.

It didn't take long for Gropper to get what little gear he had and arrange for travel out of the country. Any video surveillance of him doing anything improper would have been at night, and therefore difficult to process. His description was generic enough for any eyewitness accounts and it would change just enough with each recitation until he became just another foreigner.

If any law enforcement agency was able to connect Gropper to anything, by the time they figured it out, Gropper would already be on a plane heading back to the States. Even if Chen had betrayed him, logistically, Gropper would have too big of a head start. Besides, he didn't think Chen would sell him out; it would reveal Chen's involvement in his nephew's death, and he would never incriminate himself.

Finally, Gropper made it to the front of the queue.

"What can I get you?" a bored teenager asked. Underneath his apron, the kid wore the t-shirt of a band Gropper had never heard of. An old baseball cap with the company logo was perched on his head. The kid appeared less than enthusiastic.

"Green tea," Gropper replied.

The kid rang it up, and Gropper paid cash. He watched the kid nonchalantly get the hot water from a spigot, add the bag, and place the plastic lid on it.

"Thank you," Gropper said.

"You're welcome."

Gropper took the tea and walked to the other side of the mall. He leaned against a wall and took a sip. From here, he would take the ferry to Macau, wander around for a little while, and later take the ferry back from Macau directly to the Hong Kong airport. The boarding pass had already been printed and rested in his pocket.

He drank more tea as he considered it. From there, it would be a hop, skip, and a jump; in less than twenty-four hours, he would be home. He found a bank of payphones and typed in the number McGill had given him and an international code he'd gotten to charge to Chen. The phone rang a few times. It would be twelve hours behind where McGill was, but Gropper knew the man would be up.

"Yeah?"

"Gropper," Gropper said. "It's over. I'm heading back tonight." He could hear the sound of people in the background. "Where are you?"

"I'm at my new office," McGill replied.

CHARLESTON, SOUTH
CAROLINA 1996

BY THE TIME HE HAD GOTTEN BACK TO THE
stool, Daryl Jackson's right side around the ribcage was
decorated with welts from the laces of his opponent's
gloves. Daryl's foe kept fouling on the break. The guy
would wait until the referee's line of sight had been
compromised, and then he would scrape. It was a crafty
move the guy had probably picked up during a sparring
session with a cagey veteran.

Daryl's opponent was named Jimmy O'Farrell. He
was young, but he had already built a decent following.
Most of the crowd had cheered when the announcer
mentioned his name. Daryl imagined the meeting of
the brain trust before the fight. Jimmy and Jimmy's father, who was his manager and trainer, had probably
talked about how if they got Jimmy's record up to
twenty, maybe twenty-five, and oh, they could begin to
talk about a title shot. Shit, Jimmy had been on the un-
dercard of a televised bout already and had held a re-
gional title. A handsome kid, he was well-spoken, with
an amateur pedigree. Just serve him a few more soft
touches and start counting the money. It was only a
matter of time before he broke through and became a

main-event attraction. An undefeated record was key, though.

Both Daryl and Jimmy were represented by the same person, but it was easy to know who was being groomed for stardom. While their promoter, Doug Hanrihan, was a congenial guy who'd always treated Daryl well, and was as honest as they came, considering his profession, there had been some indications Hanrihan would prefer Jimmy get the victory. Nothing had been blatant during the build-up to the fight, like misspelling Daryl's name on the poster or anything like that, but Daryl had picked up on some subtleties. Jimmy would be easier to maneuver through the rankings for an eventual title shot. Daryl had talent, but he'd be more difficult to promote.

"The fuck are you doing?" Ray demanded after Daryl had sat on the stool. Ray's eyes were distorted from the thickness of the lenses of his glasses. Short arms were corded with veins, and his skin color bordered on obsidian. Tufts of white hair, in a Caesar-style haircut, poked from underneath a duckbill cap. Unsymmetrical patches of hair decorated his upper lip and chin.

"What round is it?" Daryl asked.

"Nine, you got one more. You better fucking do something."

Almost on cue, the referee came over and confirmed what Ray had said about the number of the upcoming round, but not the profane ultimatum.

"Hey, watch him on the breaks," Ray said to the referee, and pressed the enswell to Daryl's eye. Ray's bedside manner was lacking, but he was also one of the better trainers and cut men working. Earlier, he'd wrapped Daryl's hands in front of the Athletic Commission's representative, who signed the tape on the outside. No one from Jimmy's camp was there, although they could have been.

Once Daryl's hands were wrapped, he and Ray went to work on the mitts. There was still one fight before Daryl's, but Hanrihan wasn't one for any downtime, so if there was a knockout, Ray didn't want Daryl to be cold. They worked in sync with each other. Each shot was crisp, and a snapping noise reverberated around the cement walls of the room. The rep watched for a few moments and ducked out, probably to catch a smoke.

"Seconds out," the timekeeper announced, banged the mat, and brought Daryl out of his memory.

Ray disappeared through the ropes. Daryl stood up and adjusted his gloves. They were Reyes punchers' gloves. They had been selected by Jimmy's camp. Daryl had a reputation for a solid chin. If Jimmy knocked out Daryl, there'd be even more credibility to moving Jimmy swiftly up in the rankings.

The announcer came over the house PA and asked everyone to applaud the two fighters. A swell passed through the partisan crowd that cheered for Jimmy. It was a small venue, probably sat fifteen hundred, with maybe half of it filled, but they'd poured enough Miller Lites that the place shook when the fighters met in the center of the ring and touched gloves.

Jimmy had a smirk on his face. He was well ahead on all the cards, and he knew it. Daryl had had his moments throughout the fight, but the judges weren't going to reward his blue-collar effort. Daryl had never been a flashy fighter, and though he wasn't taking most of Jimmy's shots flush, the crowd's enthusiasm and Jimmy's panache had sold it for the judges that Jimmy was probably well ahead on the scorecards.

Daryl wasn't too worried, though. He'd been in the

game long enough to know the body shots Daryl had been landing had been taking their toll against Jimmy. Just like Meldrick Taylor had been winning his fight with Julio César Chávez by landing flashier combinations, but the bodywork Chávez had been putting in would eventually pay dividends. Chávez would win the fight by technical knockout in the final seconds of the bout.

In fact, Jimmy fouling Daryl on the break had been a telltale sign the kid had been getting frustrated. Now, at the start of the final round, they tentatively circled each other, but neither applied the pressure. Jimmy's corner had probably beaten it into him for Jimmy not to engage, since he was ahead on points.

Most likely, they said things like, "Three minutes, and you own the world" to Jimmy before sticking in his mouthpiece and sending him out for the finale. They might have pleaded with him to stay out of harm's way, a wounded animal was at its most dangerous, etcetera.

Daryl could tell Jimmy wanted to close the show and add another KO to his ledger. Jimmy kept circling away, clockwise, while Daryl stayed in the center of the ring. Daryl stopped, made a come-hither motion with his gloves, and the crowd ate it up. Daryl saw the anger at being disrespected register on the kid's face. Jimmy moved in behind two jabs and a hard right cross. Daryl ate the first, caught the second jab on his right glove, bobbed to the right, threw a jab and two left hooks to the body. He'd thrown a left hook to the body throughout the fight, but this was the first time he'd doubled it. The kid tried to counter off the first hook and took a solid shot to the liver.

Daryl didn't have to watch the rest to know how it would unfold: Jimmy would go down on both knees, rest his head on the mat like he was in prayer, the referee would stop the count at six or seven, and wave the fight off. Jimmy's corner would storm into the ring, half ready to kill him for disobeying them, but also concerned for his wellbeing. Daryl walked to his corner, rested his gloves on the top rope, and spit out his mouthpiece. He took in a few deep breaths.

Ray came over and began to cut the tape along Daryl's wrist. Daryl heard the referee make it to eight before stopping the fight.

"Fucking took you long enough," Ray said. There was more to his diatribe, but he was drowned out by the crowd.

The crowd's ardor was just starting to build, and Daryl sensed it was probably a good idea to head back to the dressing room. This was the sort of maelstrom in which brawls were borne and folding chairs were hurled along with racial epithets.

"Let's get out of here," Daryl said to Ray and darted through the ropes.

The announcer, a guy with a ponytail and multiple bejeweled broaches on his blazer, entered the ring and tried to pacify the crowd.

Daryl massaged his ribs as he walked down the corridor.

Big Ronald maneuvered the calzone in his hands and took his time to savor the smell. Some people got their nicknames ironically. Ronald did not. He was pushing three-hundred pounds, and none of it was muscle. He was also just a shade under 5'9", so he couldn't hide it like someone who weighed the same amount and was 6'7". His girth spilled out over his pants on every side. Often, he sweat profusely and felt like he was always in the process of mopping his brow with his handkerchief. It had bothered him when he was much younger; kids could be cruel, but over time he had made peace with it. He had never taken pride in his size, but it had been a long time since he had felt ashamed about it.

He knew he should take better care of himself, and he would. Next week, he would begin a serious workout regimen. He'd follow up on one of those monthly gym memberships he'd often see advertised. True, he had made these promises before, but this time he meant it. As he thought more about signing up for a complimentary session at the gym, he took a bite of the calzone. Ricotta and mozzarella cheese exploded from the side of the crusty pocket and spilled on the floor.

"Aw, shit!" he muttered.

Ronald debated whether it was worth it to get up and clean the mess. His eyes darted to his dog, Ajax, a Dutch Shepherd that lay on the floor a few feet away. The dog was in his bed and stared at the ceiling. There was always Plan B. Ronald opted for Plan B.

"Clean up," he said nonchalantly and took another bite from his calzone.

Ajax took his time but eventually rolled over onto his paws, spotted the mess on the floor, trotted to the pile, and licked up the cheese.

"Good shit, huh?" Ronald asked after the dog had finished.

The key to a good calzone was to have the place make it for you from scratch. Otherwise, they might just reheat something that had already been put together and had sat there for who knew how long. Ronald had also discovered not to let them get away with using a roll as a substitute for the usual dough.

To be fair, though, at the time he had had that realization, Ronald was hungry enough he would have eaten cardboard. So, he'd made do with the roll when the guy had said it was all they had. The pizzeria was three blocks from his house, and soon a weekly calzone became a steady part of Ronald's diet. Ajax, who had already finished the cheese and grease from the floor, now stared at Ronald. It was a look that asked if there was more in store for him. Ronald shook his head. The dog returned to his spot on the floor to continue staring at the ceiling.

Ronald was about halfway done with his calzone when the doorbell buzzed. He hesitated, put the calzone down on the grease-soaked paper plate, and rubbed his thumbs and forefingers together. He waited a few seconds longer and when silence followed, picked up the calzone again.

The buzzer rang once more, and this time Ajax started to bark.

"Aw, shit," Ronald said again.

He repositioned the calzone and tried to get up from the recliner. It took more than one attempt to gain momentum but on the third swing, he was able to make it upright.

He wiped his hands on a napkin, put on his slippers, and waddled toward the front door.

"Yeah, I'm coming," he shouted when the buzzer rang again. He undid the lock and opened the door.

Daryl Jackson greeted Ronald with a right hand to the stomach. Ronald lurched backward from the doorway. As he moved, he yelled for his dog while he spat out pieces of half-chewed calzone. The dog snapped to attention, growled, and barked a few times.

Daryl, who had moved into the entryway, shut the door behind him, and turned around just in time to turn and see the dog bound forward. Daryl put out his left arm. Ajax sank his teeth into Daryl's forearm. Daryl should have screamed and fallen to the ground, cursed The Almighty, and writhed around at mercy of the canine.

He didn't.

After a moment of struggling, the dog tore free with the arm still in his mouth. The dog shook the thing back and forth, dropped the arm, whimpered, and ran from the living room further into the apartment.

Daryl picked up his prosthetic limb and was about to re-attach it when he saw Ronald rush from the kitchen with a chef's knife. He waited for the huge man to get within a few feet and struck him in the face with the end of the false limb. It dropped Ronald where he stood.

The knife fell from Ronald's hand and clattered onto the floor. Once he was deposited on the ground, Ronald wheezed and gasped for air. Daryl waited another moment. Satisfied the coast was clear, he attached his arm, bent down, and addressed Ronald.

Daryl was not a large person, but it was difficult not to be intimidating when standing over someone after knocking them to the ground. Daryl wore a maroon t-shirt, one size too big, which masked his frame. He wasn't outwardly threatening, but he was solid, and knew how to generate power.

"Easy there, big guy. Take slow deep breaths," Daryl said.

"Fuck you, D," Ronald replied. He could barely get the words out. His chest rose and fell as his labored breathing returned.

"Serves you right," Daryl said. "Comin' at me with a knife?"

Ronald, still on his back, arched his head to look upside down toward his bedroom. "My dog's probably shitting all over the floor."

"That's what you get for siccing him on me," Daryl replied and nudged Ronald with the toe of his shoe. "And get your priorities straight," Daryl added.

Ronald groaned. "There's a book on the top shelf by the TV. It's got enough in it to cover me."

His voice sounded strained. Daryl stepped over Ronald's body and walked into the living room. A large-screen television was against one wall, with a couch and a recliner on the other side. A bookcase stood against the wall next to the television. It was empty save for the top shelf, which held only three books. Daryl quickly leafed through them.

The first two had nothing. He opened the final book,

Fat City, and a few hundred-dollar bills floated from between the pages. He returned the book to its spot and picked up the money from the floor.

Daryl walked back to the entryway. Ronald still laid sprawled out on the floor. He counted the money. "Pete told me I have to break some of your fingers."

"Really?" Ronald's voice cracked when he spoke and his eyes searched Daryl's.

Daryl added the money to a roll he kept in his pocket and returned to the bookshelf in the living room. He picked up *Fat City*, took it with him, and placed it on Ronald's stomach.

"Read this. It's good," Daryl said. "You'll have more time now."

Pete Jackson poured a few ounces worth of Jack Daniels from a bottle he kept on his desk. It was how he liked to end each day. He paused briefly to sniff the aroma and cracked open a can of Coke; he poured enough to top it off, waited for the foam to die down a little, and took a large gulp from the glass. The first drink of the day was always the best. He remembered musician James McMurtry once said it best: "I don't want another drink; I just want that last one again."

Pete took another long pull and put the glass down on his desk. He was in his office at the back of the pawnshop, which he now owned outright since his sister, Patricia, had passed. He leaned back in his chair and looked around the room.

A framed picture of him and Patricia was one of the few things he'd kept on the desktop, along with the bottle. The photo had been taken a long time ago, when they were both much younger, back when Pete had curly black hair. Now his hair was white, which he wore short, so it was easier to manage. He looked fit for someone who was sixty-five, something which hadn't changed since his youth. He had also been told, on more than one occasion, his resemblance to Louis Gossett Jr. was uncanny.

He was a veteran of two tours in Vietnam. When he had returned home to Charleston, he had been disillusioned, and he was uncertain of what he should do with his time. Many of his friends had gotten caught up in one or more of the various movements, which had continued to gain traction in his absence. He hadn't felt compelled to join any of them … probably the reason why he'd ended up working for his father.

Pete's father, Victor, hadn't been a career criminal by any stretch, but he had begun to dabble in bookmaking. Someone had placed a wager with Pete's old man, and the guy had been delinquent with his payment when he had lost the bet. So, one day, Victor Jackson had asked his son, Peter, to visit this acquaintance. It only took a single face-to-face meeting for the man to pay up.

From that point on, for as long as the man continued to do business with Pete's father, he had never been late with another payment. Once Victor realized his son would be a worthwhile enforcer, he immediately brought him into the fold. It wasn't long before Pete started to make frequent trips to visit people who had trouble coming up with the money they owed. Pete remembered often listening to the old man tell a long-winded story about the nature of their business, and the derivation of most of the terms. "The vigorish, or the vig,"—his father had said many times—"is the amount we charge for our services." Pete still remembered his father's exact words. "It's Jewish slang for 'winnings'."

During the years which followed, Pete and Patricia—who had also started to work for the old man—learned the ropes. Pete became a more visible part of the organization whereas Patricia was value added behind the scenes. She had a knack for math. Similarly, Pete and Patricia also learned how to use the pawnshop to facilitate their business. People always had items to pawn, wagers to make, and money to spend. Even during more turbulent times, when the job market was in disarray, gas prices had increased, and drugs flooded the streets, their business prospered.

Pete and Patricia took over after a while and, eventually, Pete ran things on his own. Since his divorce, Pete had practically lived at the shop. He took another sip of his drink. Aside from the bottle and the photo on the desk, there was a stereo system and some boxing memorabilia which hung from the wall. His office was located just off a hallway. To the right of his office was the door for the back exit, and the hallway to the left fed into the front stock room, which housed all the merchandise. A long counter stood a few feet from the back wall of that room, which had been lined with shelves to display everything from appliances to musical instruments.

He put the cap back on the Jack Daniels bottle and left it on the desk. He could have kept the bottle in a drawer or a cooler but leaving it on the desk reminded him of one of his favorite lines from a movie.

"One thing I like working for myself. I always have a bottle on the table." The line had been spoken by a gangster in the film *Devil in a Blue Dress*.

Pete opened the top drawer, rummaged around, pushed aside a snub-nosed .22, and grabbed a few bills. He placed the money on the desk and killed his drink.

The man seated across the table reached over and picked up the stack. He pocketed the money without looking at it.

"Did he give you any trouble?" Pete asked.

"No."

Daryl hadn't hesitated when he spoke, but Pete could tell there was more.

"I know he's your friend and all," Pete said.

"I didn't hold back," Daryl stated.

Pete ceased his line of questions. He knew Daryl had been uncomfortable with the whole arrangement, but business was business, and Ronald had started to press his bets to cover his losses.

Even while seated, Daryl still gave off the impression he was still quick. His years boxing had taught him how to move with a certain fluidity that had never left him. Pete knew it was one of the reasons Daryl had been such an effective collector, even after the loss of an arm.

"You know, I could always hand his debt off to someone else," Pete said casually.

"That doesn't make sense," Daryl said almost immediately and went into business mode. His face was blank. "You'd only get 40 cents on the dollar for it. Maybe."

Pete nodded slowly as the warmth of the drink spread through his body. "Well, you've done good. How's the arm been treating you?"

Daryl glanced down at his prosthetic limb. "It's fine."

"Good," Pete said. "I need you to pay a visit to Jose Rodriguez tonight."

"Okay."

Daryl headed out the door and left Pete to his own devices. Pete didn't wait much longer before he poured himself a second drink. He topped off his glass and opened the second drawer down from his desk. He removed the newspaper clipping that had now yellowed around the edges.

Pete read the article again, even though he practically had it memorized. He put it back in the drawer before he had gotten to the part where the writer speculated the boxer might have to have his arm amputated.

Pete finished his drink.

He took a remote control from the top drawer and pushed a button. The stereo started to play and soon the sounds of De La Soul filled the room. Before she had died, his sister Patricia had made Pete promise he would take care of her son, Daryl. Pete had kept his word. He had slept in the hospital room before and after Daryl's surgery. Pete would never forget how his nephew looked when he was in recovery, attached to multiple machines like a robot. It was incredible he'd survived in the first place. The car accident had claimed the lives of three of the five people involved immediately after the crash.

Daryl had been riding in the backseat, which had been the deciding factor in preserving his life. Of course, there had been complications that led to the loss of his arm ... and the end of his career as a prizefighter.

McGill drank more of his coffee. He added cream to take some of the edge off, but the caffeine had ceased working hours ago. He'd forgotten which number cup it was he was currently drinking. He usually lost count at some point in the early morning. Now that it was the late afternoon, he could understand people's fascination with his coffee intake since he drank enough to "blind an ox", as someone once put it.

He spotted Gropper walking past the group of servers who'd gathered by the front to mark the end of their shift. Gropper silently took his seat, and a waiter came by with a cup of green tea. Gropper thanked him, and the waiter departed.

"How's everything?" McGill asked.

"It's fine."

McGill paused as the waiter returned to fill his coffee. When the waiter left, McGill spoke. "Glad to hear it."

Gropper had continued to stay with the Hares after he and McGill had returned the kodachi short sword to Lawrence Crider. Unfortunately, Mr. Hare had been unable to continue joining Gropper and McGill at the diner; over the last few weeks, his health had deteriorated. It had gotten to the point where he would probably have to be moved to an assisted living facility.

The elder Hare had been a welcome addition to McGill and Gropper's meetings at the diner. Art Hare had brought a certain levity with him, and neither McGill or Gropper ever tired of hearing Hare's stories, whether they focused on his life in the Marine corps or as a younger man in West Virginia. Regardless, though, everything continued to move forward.

McGill thought of Renee for the first time in a long while.

"What's on your mind?" Gropper said.

The door to The Oasis Bar & Grill opened, and Daryl walked inside. The music was loud but it wasn't overpowering. The place was relatively empty except for the bartender and a middle-aged man in a wrinkled suit, who looked like he'd been brined.

Daryl sauntered to the bar, ordered a shot of Jameson and a beer chaser. He leaned in and spoke to the bartender as she poured his shot. She had to move in closer to hear him over the music, and nodded yes to his question and motioned toward the back. Daryl did his shot and took a long pull of his beer.

He made his way past the empty tables to a hallway in the back, which led to the parking lot. Outside, two people were busy enjoying a smoke. They stopped their conversation when they saw Daryl .

"Damn it," said the taller one.

He was Latino, had a Fu-Manchu mustache, and long hair. He wore a Megadeth t-shirt that depicted some sort of zombie wielding a bloody ax. The word "Killers" was written in red off to the side. The other one was a heavyset Latino with a full beard; he wore a Slayer t-shirt. It depicted the band's logo in white, set across a pentagram made of connecting sword blades. He looked at his friend, arched an eyebrow, and took another drag. The guy with the Fu-Manchu wore an apron, the standard uniform of grill operators.

"Rodriguez," Daryl said to the tall one with the Fu-Manchu. His tone suggested this was a social call.

Based on Rodriguez's exclamation, though, it sounded like anything but.

"You got the four dimes you owe me?" Daryl added.

"Shit, you know I'm good for it. You didn't have to come down here," Rodriguez said.

The friend took a step forward and started speaking Spanish. *"Pocos pero locos, cabron."*

"Easy, Luis," Rodriguez said to his friend. He turned back to Daryl .

"You sure you wanna do this, man? Luis's connected," Rodriguez said. There dawas an edge to his voice now.

"You been ducking Pete's calls."

He killed his beer and threw the bottle in a nearby trash can full of cigarette butts. No one said anything for a moment. Rodriguez suddenly started to laugh. He took a final drag of his cigarette and flicked the butt at Daryl 's chest. Sparks exploded when it landed.

"Fuck you," Rodriguez said.

Daryl had already started to move, closed the gap between them quickly, and landed an overhand right to Rodriguez's chin. The sound echoed around the parking lot. The tall Latino fell where he stood.

Luis was still for a moment, but only a moment. He opened a gravity knife and yelled, *"Pinche mayate!"*

Daryl brought up his left arm to block the attack, and Luis stabbed him in the forearm. Luis took a step back, dumbfounded, and Daryl landed a two-punch combination with his right hand: an uppercut and right hook. Luis fell to the ground. Somehow, he was still conscious. He rattled off another diatribe in Spanish.

Daryl pulled the knife from his forearm, shut the blade, and threw it in the trash. He walked over to Rodriguez, who had begun to stir. He brought his foot down on one of Rodriguez's hands. The crunch of breaking bones was audible. Rodriguez let out a scream and gripped his hand.

Daryl went through Rodriguez's pockets and took out a wallet. "Sixty? That's it?" Daryl took it all and kicked Rodriguez in the ribs. He dropped the wallet on Rodriguez, turned, and delivered a kick into Luis. The man's body vibrated as he took the shot, and he let out a bellow before he passed out. Daryl looked back and forth at his handiwork and scanned the parking lot, but it was still too early for there to be a crowd.

"Don't make me come back here," Daryl warned before he walked away.

"Conflict of interest," McGill said, sipped his coffee, and relayed the conversation to Gropper that McGill had had earlier in the day.

Ivan had been a former client and had subsequently become one of McGill's friends. Sheldon, Ivan's son, had been trying to rehabilitate his life. Sheldon had recently been paroled. As someone who'd been a gifted artist as a youth, sculpting was a trade Sheldon had wanted to revisit once he got back into the world. He was able to open a store selling original sculptures, as well as handmade jewelry. The jewelry had been crafted by local artisans who also ran a stall at the Strawmarket. They would give Sheldon merchandise to sell in the store, but Sheldon was in charge of the sculptures.

He was proficient in a few mediums—such as clay and cast iron—and, so far, the business had been profitable. Sheldon had also been able to keep his nose clean. He'd continued to check in every week with his parole officer and had yet to incur any infractions. However, he wasn't able to get a loan from any banks to fund his store; his criminal record would always come up and derail any sort of progress.

Letters that highlighted Sheldon's immaculate behavior while behind bars and after his parole could not sway bank management to extend him a loan. Therefore, with little recourse, Sheldon got the money through other means.

"As you can imagine, Sheldon's having trouble paying back the points on the loan."

Loans from people who operated under the table were usually skewed heavily in favor of the lender. Most of the demands were impossible to meet.

"Who's applying the pressure?" Gropper asked.

"Pete Jackson."

There it was. Pete and McGill had done business in the

past, and Pete had proven to be a great asset. He would always tip McGill and Gropper on any hot items someone had tried to pawn at the shop he owned and operated.

A waiter brought over a plate of French fries for McGill.

"What are you thinking?" Gropper asked.

McGill's face sank a little.

"I told Ivan I'd see what I could do."

Gropper nodded. One of the only stipulations Pete had in working with McGill was assurance that neither McGill nor Gropper would interfere in any of Pete's operations, legal or illegal.

"I could talk to Daryl," Gropper said.

McGill finished his coffee and instantly got a refill. Daryl and Gropper had never crossed paths before when it came to business. Both had respected the other's abilities, though.

"If it's coming from me instead of you," Gropper added.

McGill sucked at his teeth as he contemplated the idea and called over the waiter to order another entree. "Okay, see what Daryl thinks."

***

Mojo had flown into the Charleston airport in the early afternoon. He could probably have driven, but he didn't want to have to focus. He tried to relax on the flight, but he always had trouble keeping calm before handling business. It didn't matter. Soon enough, he would be back home and have all the time in the world to relax. He knew he could have stayed in Florida and continued to oversee things from the comfort of home, but he also knew if he didn't take a hands-on role, then plans could deviate. He couldn't afford to be an armchair quarterback like his predecessor; that had led to Hector's downfall.

After Hector had been killed, some of the more vocal constituency wanted immediate retribution—especially since Hector's assassin had come to Miami to finish business. However, the decision was made to do more research before a contract was opened and they settled the account, so to speak.

When enough time had passed, and the opportunity finally came, Mojo welcomed the chance to orchestrate the revenge. Hector had been Mojo's cousin, so it was also personal. Mojo was probably being too cautious with his planning, but he wasn't going to take this Gropper person lightly; Gropper had proven himself more than capable when he took care of La Espada.

Even at an advanced age, La Espada had been a force to be reckoned with; there were bodies in the morgue full of people who'd underestimated La Espada. Not to mention, Gropper had bested La Espada with a knife. Mojo wasn't going to take Gropper lightly, even if it seemed like overkill.

Mojo stepped off the moving sidewalk, navigated through the crowd that was waiting to retrieve baggage from the carousel, and walked to the rental car counter. He spoke with a woman who looked like she'd been convicted of a crime, and her job with the rental agency had been part of her sentence. Within minutes, he was fiddling with the controls of the rented Hyundai. He adjusted the seat and rearview mirrors, attached his seatbelt, and left the airport parking lot. He'd researched how it was the most popular type of rental car, and though he didn't anticipate having to make a quick or memorable getaway, he didn't want to leave anything to chance.

As he drove along the highway to his motel, Mojo recalled the difficulties in tracking down Gropper.

NCIC, the National Crime Information Center, facial-recognition software had come up empty. It was as if Hector's assailant ceased to exist. It had taken a computer hacker days to piece together still photos from traffic stops, which had eventually led them to Gropper and Charleston. By the time the search had ended, some of the bosses had almost cooled on the decision to open the contract on their mystery man. However, once they had gotten a name and remembered what had happened to Hector, and how much of an insult it had been, it took little prompting. Mojo was given the go-ahead.

The GPS spoke and brought Mojo out of the recollection. He turned off the highway and into the parking lot of the hotel. He would check into his room, drop off his stuff, shower, and meet his contact at the restaurant later in the evening.

Mojo exited the car, stretched, and approached the entrance to check-in. After he relaxed, he would meet a local who would serve as his guide and liaison. Mojo opened the door to the lobby and met the cool breeze from an air conditioning unit on high. He paid cash for his room and said he'd be staying for three nights. There would be no problem in adding additional time to his stay if it was needed. He thanked the man behind the desk, took his key, walked through the lobby, and passed the elevator bank to his room.

Again, while he didn't think it would be necessary, it was an old habit to get a room on the ground floor in case he needed to make a quick escape. However, he wasn't going to tempt fate. It was one thing to contemplate whether he was being too cautious versus needing to make an expedited retreat and being stuck on the tenth floor.

Mojo moved his carry-on bag into the closet but didn't unpack. He checked the time. He was supposed to meet his contact in an hour, so he would have enough time to do a light workout and take a shower.

Part of Mojo's daily workout included a thousand push-ups a day. He knocked out another hundred and circled the room until his heart rate had slowed. His endorphins continued to release their magic elixir.

He finished his last set of fifty, stood up, and wiped off his hands. His musculature wasn't incredibly defined. He wouldn't have graced the layout of a fitness magazine. However, that made little difference. When he finished, Mojo went to the bathroom. One of Mojo's former cellmates had been Muslim and since the man had frequently prayed within the cell, they had agreed to only use the toilet while seated.

Even years after he had been released, Mojo couldn't go to the bathroom without sitting down.

Gropper left the diner and got into his car. He'd go see Daryl at the pawnshop this evening, but he still had plenty of time. Since Mr. Hare had begun to deteriorate, Gropper started to consider a new living arrangement. He also had a desire to check in on Connie and Liz, though Connie was working a new shift, and Liz wouldn't be home till much later; she had dance practice right after school. Her team had won regionals and, in doing so, qualified for nationals. So, for the next few weeks, both Liz and Connie would be busy this time of day.

Gropper pulled out of the diner's parking lot and continued his weekly routine. Each day, he would take care of a few different tasks. Today, he drove to the bus stop, where he checked his locker, made sure his go-bag was ready, and took any weapons with him which needed to be cleaned.

The radio station he'd grown fond of over the last few years was having a retrospective on Cannonball Adderley. He drove around to various dead-drops where he collected payments that had been owed him and McGill for services rendered. Although some clients preferred to pay McGill at the diner, others were more comfortable if money didn't directly change hands. Gropper arrived at the last spot he'd need to check: the sidewalk drain at a dead-end street. He pulled the car to a stop and waited for the final section of "Mercy, Mercy, Mercy". When the song finished and the disc jockey began his final summation of the retrospective, Gropper got out of the car. He bent down by the drain, reached in his hand and felt for the envelope which would be on the ledge. He removed it, took it to the car, and put it in the glove compartment with the others. The retrospective on Cannonball Adderley had finished, but next up was a selection of some personal favorites of great soundtracks. They were going to kick things off with "Round Midnight" and included in the rotation would be tracks from "Elevator to The Gallows", "Blow-Up", and "Anatomy of a Murder".

Gropper had had to rid himself of certain weapons over the years, but he had also added to his arsenal. He opened the kitbag on the passenger seat, removed a whetstone, some mineral oil, and one of his most recent acquisitions, a Gerber automatic knife. He lubricated the stone with the oil, put it back in the kitbag, and opened the blade. He spent the next twenty minutes sharpening the edge, then checked the time. Neither Liz nor Connie would be back for another hour or so.

After he returned the kitbag to his locker at the bus station, rather than return home to the Hares, Gropper decided to visit the cemetery and pay his respects. The cemetery was close by, and there hadn't been any traffic. Gropper listened to songs from Miles Davis and Thelonious Monk. In fact, he waited until "Straight No Chaser" ended before he emerged from the car.

The cemetery was empty, but it still didn't stop Gropper from checking the perimeter. While he had certainly softened in the last few years, there were some old habits which he could never get rid of. He got out of the car, entered the cemetery, and walked over to the section that housed Ms. Bradley's headstone.

Gropper hadn't known Ms. Bradley had been sick until he read her obituary. He'd only seen her once or twice since he'd moved out of her spare room. He recalled many of the times they would sit in rocking chairs on her front porch or listen to records in her living room. It was a completely different experience than the relationship he'd had with Mr. Hare, but it was just as enjoyable. Though Gropper had wished he'd been able to see her before she passed, he also didn't want her or her family to have to endure any collateral damage if sometime had tried to visit retribution on him.

Of all the aspects of Gropper's code, being transitory and able to move at a moment's notice was extremely important. While he no longer took as many alternate routes to get to familiar places and ignored other rules he'd previously established—such as finally getting a cell phone—being able to move freely was something he still valued.

Gropper picked up a stone from the ground and left it on top Ms. Bradley's headstone.

"Would you like to order?" the waitress asked.

She wore too much eyeshadow, which gave her the appearance of a depressed person. She popped her chewing gum as if to further express her displeasure. This was the second time she had asked Mojo whether he would like to order. The first time, he had told her that he would wait for his guest but now, as he glanced around the empty restaurant, he figured he'd give her something to do.

"A Tecate," Mojo said after a cursory glance at the menu.

"Sure thing," she said and quickly turned away. The sound of her gum popping reverberated around the room. Mojo went back to watching the fish swim in the tank nearby. They were mesmerizing in the same way meditation often provided comfort.

Those he chose to tell were often surprised to learn of his meditation practice. He had heard all the rumors about him throughout the years, and they never stopped amazing him. It was a job. He just happened to have a certain aptitude for it. There were those, like La Espada, who had a taste for violence but often turned out to be a hazard in the end. Usually, people thought of scenes from movies about assassins who were mentally unstable and got a twisted pleasure from hurting others. Though many of them existed, and some even prospered, most were eventually caught or killed because they would lose sight of their perspective.

Mojo didn't enjoy the work. If people had known half the things about him—he was married, had children, paid taxes. Let people think what they wanted. It only helped to keep him shrouded in mystery ... and mystery was *always* better.

The waitress reappeared with the Tecate, which she placed on the table. Mojo drank some of the beer and checked the time. His local contact should arrive momentarily. Mojo had never met the guy, but people had vouched for him.

And, almost on cue, the guy showed up. Mojo

nodded to the man who made his way to the table and took a seat. He was heavyset with a beard. One side of his face was decorated from a bruise, vivid purple and yellow, and he favored one side as he sat down.

"*Soy* Luis," the man said.

Luis had mostly recovered from his run-in the other night. He still sported some bruises, and he didn't have full range of motion yet, but he'd find the guy who'd beaten him and Jose. Luis had already picked up the piece: a snub-nosed .38.

Luis had been watching *Taxi Driver* at the time he was considering getting a firearm, and there was a scene in the movie when one of the characters was selling guns, showed a .38, and said, You"could go out and hammer nails with it all day. Come back, and it'll hit dead center every time." That's what Luis needed. Something accurate.

He wasn't going to spend time on the gun range, and he didn't need anything that would drop the engine out of a car. He imagined how the scene would play out in his head. He'd find Daryl, wait until the guy was alone, walk up, and say something clever like, "Not so tough now." Then, he'd unload the clip.

Luis would have put duct tape on the trigger and handle, and he would let the weapon fall from his hand as he left the scene—just like in *The Godfather*, when Michael Corleone had been instructed by Clemenza, a capo in the family, about taking revenge by killing the corrupt cop who'd broken his jaw. The more Luis thought about it, the more he looked forward to re-enacting the scenes. However, before he could do that, he needed to take care of business.

Luis's cousin, Esteban, had called him a few days

previously. Esteban wasn't a high-ranking member of the syndicate, but he did have juice. So, when he asked if Luis would drive Mojo around while he handled business, it was more of a command than a question. Luis practically jumped at the opportunity.

Mojo? Mojo. El Magico? The man was a legend. Initially, Luis had thought Mojo was code for a team of people. It seemed impossible for one man to cause half the carnage that had solidified Mojo's reputation.

Luis assured Estaban that he could help in any way possible, and had been given the time and place to meet Mojo: at some restaurant near downtown Charleston. Luis was surprised at how unassuming Mojo looked. After confirming it was him, Luis sat, and ordered nachos. He'd anticipated someone like The Terminator or Juggernaut, a completely different person from who Mojo turned out to be.

Mojo had none of the qualities or traits of those two characters. Mojo wasn't larger than life. In fact, when they both stood to head to the car, Luis was an inch or two taller than Mojo.

He was careful to note the way Mojo moved throughout the restaurant, in case there was a hint of preternatural ability, but he didn't notice anything out of the ordinary. They climbed into Luis's car. Mojo took the passenger seat and Luis reached into the glove compartment and retrieved a gravity knife in a case which he had picked up along with the .38.

He'd wanted to give Mojo the knife as a gift.

"*Gracias,*" Mojo said, and put the knife in his pocket. He took out a half dollar and gave it to Luis, explaining the reasoning behind giving a coin in exchange for a knife.

As Luis listened to Mojo explain the folklore behind the gesture, he realized he had been a fool to assume Mojo was going to be a larger-than-life character. Those sorts of things were best left to the movies.

"Where to?" Luis asked and turned the ignition.

"He frequents a diner," Mojo replied.

The bass guitar was still in the case. It hadn't been moved from the pawnshop's counter yet, and it was open to reveal everything: the instrument and all its accessories. Pete had just hung up the phone with Leonard who—as Leonard had said the last three times this had happened—would be by in ten minutes to make the arrangements to purchase the instrument.

Leonard was the guitarist for a band named Dread Medicine. At one point, the members of the band had thought of messing around with the spelling. It was the same reason the band Led Zeppelin had taken out the "a", so there wouldn't be any confusion in the pronunciation of the band's name. The drummer, Stephen, had suggested the name Shotgun Money Killers. In the end, they decided to keep it simple and stuck with Dread Medicine. Stephen acquiesced but said they should leave the letter "a" in the band name.

Stephen had explained that people might be think the band was named after Dred Scott, a former slave who sued for his freedom and lost a landmark Supreme Court case. People might also think the band was going to play music influenced by the fictional character, Judge Dredd, a law enforcement officer in a future dystopian United States. Rather than argue with Stephen about the potential for people to be confused with such esoteric examples, they stayed with the original spelling. The band had been signed to an independent label, but most people who'd heard them thought they would be destined for bigger things in the future.

The front door of the pawnshop opened, and Leonard entered. He walked up to the counter, saw the instrument, and sighed. He looked spent and weathered, and looked much healthier during previous meetings. He had always seemed put together: clean clothes, combed hair, and a generally pleasant disposition, even though his dealings with Pete were less than desirable. However, Pete could tell these episodes were beginning to take their toll on Leonard. Aside from making sure the band didn't implode, Leonard was also managing their career until a suitable replacement could be found. Now, he wore a ripped plain white t-shirt, jeans, and looked like he'd just been awakened from a deep sleep.

"I'm sorry," Leonard said.

Pete didn't respond. At this point, there wasn't anything Pete could say that hadn't already been said during the previous conversations. Leonard nodded a few times as if he understood Pete's silence and began to pack up the guitar.

The instrument belonged to the primary songwriter, bass player, singer, and inspiration of the group: Monica. Over the last year, she had developed a debilitating opiate addiction. The band had always dabbled in something, but eventually Monica went off the rails. Ultimately, she would pawn her guitar, the only thing of value she possessed anymore and use the money to score.

Reliably, Monica would show up at Pete's. It got to the point where he could set his watch by it. They wouldn't haggle at all. He would give her a few hundred dollars and immediately call Leonard, who would come directly to the shop to buy back the guitar. While no one liked the way the scenario developed, at least this way they could stay on top of everything. They had tried an intervention before, which had seemed to work. She had gone to rehab, twice, and the second time everyone thought it had taken—until, of course, it hadn't.

The telltale signs had been difficult to see, but soon it became obvious to everyone she was using again. Her family and bandmates had gone through all the stages and now they figured as long as they could keep it contained, that was the best they could do. They knew she would pawn her instrument to Pete. It was the only known variable, and they would have to make do with that.

When things had been at their lowest point, Pete had suggested Daryl visit her, but upon reflection realized she couldn't be forced; Monica needed to arrive at the decision to quit drugs on her own.

The second time she pawned her instrument, Pete had been overcome with emotion. Monica wasn't high, but she had been clearly going through withdrawal. Pete had known her since she had been a little kid, and to see her in this position made him feel the same vulnerability he'd felt when Daryl had been in the hospital. Pete wanted to grab Monica by the shoulders. He hadn't done that. Instead, he had given her the cash she had asked for and allowed her to be on her way. His guess was she would go directly to her dealer. Again, he thought of sending Daryl to visit the dealer, but that would have been a waste of time. Monica was determined.

That time, when Leonard had arrived to retrieve Monica's bass, Pete had confessed as if Leonard were a priest who could give Pete absolution. Leonard and everyone else had already absolved Pete of any wrongdoing, but Pete still felt the need to rid himself of his guilt as he felt he'd somehow been complicit in her downward spiral.

Now, Pete barely registered emotion when Monica

showed up. During previous visits, she would try to explain herself, suggest everything was under control, that even though she'd had some difficulty with how things had played out, she could handle it.

However, this time, she stayed quiet. There would be no way for her to argue things were fine in her current state. Aside from her pale complexion and dishevelled appearance, she had begun to exhibit certain vocal tics when she spoke. Rather than offer any excuses, or try to deny she had a problem, she simply left the instrument on the counter and put her hand out for the payment. Instead of beginning a lecture or engaging in a tirade, Pete counted out the bills and handed them over. When the exchanges first happened, he gave her the claim ticket for the item, but now he simply saved it for Leonard.

The phone rang and Pete answered.

"I know your address, and I'm coming to pay you a visit, motherfucker," the voice said.

Pete sighed. Though the caller was angry, the man hadn't yelled. However, the caller had spoken to Pete through gritted teeth, and Pete knew the person had been gripping the phone so tightly, he was on the verge of crushing the device.

"You're looking for ADA Cohen; you got the wrong number."

The line went dead.

Someone had written the pawnshop phone number on the wall of the country detention center. Originally, it had been attributed to a bail bond company, so for a few months, Pete would field calls inquiring about bail.

Later, someone had written the name of an assistant district attorney above the phone number. The DA seemed to have a pretty sizable fan club. One evening, Pete took a phone call from a concerned father who began the conversation with a tirade of how he was going to take revenge against Cohen and his whole office.

The man, a Mr. Cobb, said his son, who'd been railroaded by Cohen, had proudly served in Iraq. The Cobb family had a cache of firearms and the elder Cobb swore he'd see justice done. Pete spoke to Mr. Cobb for a few minutes and was able to explain the mix-up in telephone numbers. Pete also suggested Mr. Cobb not continue his mission, or at least not to call the assistant district attorney to issue threats.

It was soon after that, Pete learned about the graffiti. Pete called the detention center and spoke to the duty sergeant, who confirmed the phone number had been written on the wall and assured Pete he would have someone scrub it off. However, the calls kept coming, so Pete wasn't so sure the sergeant ever got around to doing it.

The phone rang again. This time it was Daryl .

"Anything collections for this evening?" Daryl asked.

"Yeah, I worked out a payment plan with Ronald to cover the balance," Pete replied.

"OK," Daryl said.

"He also wanted me to let you know he's enjoying *Fat City*."

"Sounds good. I'll pay him a visit, and I'll see you later tonight."

Pete hung up and retired to his office to pour himself a stiff drink.

Luis hadn't realized exactly how much of the job was simply waiting around. He knew it wasn't going to be a non-stop shoot 'em up, but they'd gotten to the diner a half an hour ago and were waiting in the parking lot. Mojo had showed Luis a photograph of the man they were looking for and explained how they were just gathering information at this point. Mojo went on to suggest how important knowing the information would be to creating a plan.

For someone who had an impressive mythology, Mojo hadn't met any of Luis's expectations, but at least he had let Luis go inside the diner and order some food to go. Luis had eaten at the Mexican restaurant, but he was hungry again, and just knowing they were frying things on the grill made him anxious. He took a drink of his Coke and fidgeted in his seat again. The plastic bag and Styrofoam container by his feet crinkled when he came into contact with them.

"I know," Mojo said casually. "Not what you were hoping for."

It caught Luis off guard, and before he could answer, he'd already hemmed and hawed.

"This is ninety percent of the job," Mojo said, then took out his wallet and a Polaroid photo from inside the billfold. "This is the other ten."

Luis had wanted to look away, but he was captivated by the sheer audacity of the carnage.

"Sometimes, the client wants a trophy," Mojo added.

"*Entiendo*," Luis said and relaxed in his seat. He didn't realize it until he saw his face in the mirror, but he had begun to sweat.

Daryl could hear the television in the living room when he got to Ronald's front door. He pressed the bell and waited. He heard the dog bark a few times, then come to the door and bang against it.

"One second," Ronald said.

Daryl heard feet approaching.

"Who is it?" Ronald said. From inside, the voice was muffled, but it had gotten clearer when he'd reached the front door.

"It's Daryl."

"Oh," Ronald said.

The chain was on, so the door only opened a few inches.

Once the dog confirmed who it was, he turned and scurried to another room. The door shut, the chain was removed, and the door opened again.

"Gimme one second," Ronald said. He disappeared into the living room and returned with an envelope, which he handed to Daryl. Ronald's right arm was in a cast to his elbow with the plaster extended to the ring and pinky fingers.

Both men acknowledged the injury, but neither said anything. The dog whined from the next room.

"Thank you," Daryl said, held up the envelope, and put it in his pocket.

"No problem."

"See you next week."

"You got it—oh, wait," Ronald said quickly.

"Yeah?"

"I told Ray I'd seen you. He asked for you to call him when you can."

Daryl kept the shame from his face, nodded, and told Ronald he'd call Ray as soon as he could. Ronald shut the door and locked it. Daryl heard Ronald assuring his dog everything would be OK.

Daryl sat in the car outside of Floyd's gym. He tried to remember the last time he'd been inside, but it had been years. He also attempted to recall the last time he'd seen or spoken to Ray, and he couldn't remember that either. The last time they'd spoken, both had said some pretty despicable things to each other. This time, Daryl could have called, but it wasn't like Ray to suddenly reach out like this, so whatever he wanted to talk about with Daryl had to be something monumental. Daryl made his way to the front and pressed the buzzer.

A voice answered from the callbox, "Yeah?"

"It's Daryl."

Ray lived in a small room above the gym. He'd purchased it outright from Floyd when Daryl was still in contention for a possible title shot. At the time, there were three fighters in Ray's stable who he had been developing: a flyweight, lightweight, and Daryl at welterweight. Unfortunately, none of them reached the Promised Land. Of course, Daryl's car accident had ended his career. The flyweight had never fully realized his potential, and the lightweight had signed with another manager/trainer.

Ray hadn't trained a professional in a long time. Instead, he conducted a few classes and occasionally helped an individual client get in shape.

"Be right there," the voice answered from the callbox.

Daryl felt a rush of adrenalin. It had been a long time since that had happened. A few moments later, the door opened. Ray still looked the same. Some of his hair had thinned, but otherwise it was the same Ray.

"Come in." Ray stepped back, and Darryl walked inside.

The layout of the gym was the same: a ring to the right, some heavy bags to the left, and other equipment in the back.

Ray shut the door. "How long's it been?"

Daryl expected the hammer to drop, and for Ray to let loose with all sorts of deplorable expletives, but Ray stayed silent.

The main room still had the overpowering smell of Ben Gay and liniment rub. Most of the equipment looked like it needed to be upgraded, but still fit the decor. Ray motioned for Daryl to follow him to the office just beyond the heavy bags.

Ray turned on the light and took a seat behind the desk. Daryl immediately saw the framed poster on the wall to the left and stared. It was the poster for Daryl's fight against Jimmy O'Farrell.

"Better days," Ray said.

Daryl took a seat.

"Look, I wanna make some things right," Ray added. He was going to get right into it, no small talk, no catching up. "The doctor gave me six months to a year ..."

Daryl nodded.

"I said some things—"

"We both did," Daryl interjected.

It was Ray's turn to nod.

They caught up for about twenty minutes, then Daryl saw what time it was on the clock on the wall. "Look, I gotta get going," Daryl said. "But I'll be back tomorrow, OK?"

"Sounds good." Ray stood and walked Daryl to his car.

During the drive, Daryl attempted to process what he'd just learned, and although he didn't want to revisit their falling out, it was impossible not to think about it. Daryl knew deep down that Ray hadn't known how to deal with the end of Daryl's career. Ray had offered to bring him into the mix, have him teach a class, train other boxers, but Daryl didn't have the desire for the sport anymore.

Daryl had tried to explain to Ray that he intended to work for his Uncle Pete, that it wasn't about fulfilling an urge to hurt people. He spoke about obligation to family and more, but Ray wasn't having any of it.

Each man took turns unloading both barrels. In the end, it was a burned bridge that could only be salvaged by time.

Luis had noticed the man, Gropper, arrive at the diner. And although Mojo had already taken note, it was a sign Luis had been paying attention. Mojo understood Luis's disillusionment with waiting around in a parking lot. Mojo had conditioned himself to adapt to whatever the job required, but he also knew he had a unique skillset. While Luis was still very green and rough around the edges, he had demonstrated a willingness to learn.

Gropper went into the diner, and a beat passed.

"Do we follow him?" Luis asked.

"No," Mojo replied.

"OK." There was still a lingering desire to want to act; that much was apparent in Luis's tone, but he had calmed down significantly.

In a few minutes, Gropper reappeared and went to his car.

"*Now* we follow him," Mojo said.

Before they pulled out, Mojo gave Luis a quick tutorial on how far back to stay. Mojo knew Gropper would probably make his tail; the man was too skilled, even if Luis was a seasoned professional. However, Mojo was going to change cars tomorrow anyway, so it didn't matter.

Gropper pulled into the parking spot, turned off the engine, and stayed in the car to finish listening to Wes Montgomery. Before the host of the program had played the next track, he spent some time discussing how Montgomery's unique style of guitar playing had developed from his attempt to play softly, so he wouldn't bother his neighbors when he practiced. Gropper had planned to exit the car as soon as the host finished his story, but the man played "Too Late Now" next and Gropper realized he'd have to wait for the song to finish before he could leave. This was not a hard and fast rule, but he knew he would regret it later if he cut the song short.

A few minutes elapsed and now satisfied, Gropper exited the car. The fluorescent light of Jackson's Pawnshop was off, but the inside light still burned. Not to mention, Daryl's car was parked out front. Gropper hummed the last few bars of "'Round Midnight" as he walked to the front door.

———

Gropper had pulled in front of a pawnshop in a strip mall, so Mojo told Luis to keep going and pull in a few storefronts over. There was a supermarket with plenty of spaces. Luis shut off the ignition. Earlier, he would have asked about the next move but now he sat, ready to be given instructions. He was learning. Mojo checked the time and looked over at the front of the pawnshop.

There were one or two cowboys among the higher-ups who would approve a reckless retaliation. If Mojo called and told them he had a definite location of the target, he could probably get the authorization to pull the trigger. Why not have someone go in with a machine gun and simply spray the place? Sure, you might kill some staff and patrons, but wasn't that the cost of doing business?

At this point, though, there was no need for any unnecessary collateral damage, especially if it could be avoided. Why entice the FBI or the DEA to get involved? Mojo made a note to check the pawnshop to see whether it was a front for anything.

"Feel like checking out some merchandise?" Mojo asked Luis.

Luis hadn't realized he'd been holding his breath. He exhaled slowly and felt the exhilaration culminate in a single word. "Yes."

He further confirmed with Mojo that he understood he was not to engage their target. Luis would go inside and make sure their guy was still in there. It wasn't beyond the realm of possibilities that Gropper had taken a back exit. Even though Gropper's car was still parked out front, that didn't mean anything. If Gropper was still inside, Luis could linger, pretend to check to see what items might look interesting, and then depart. That was it.

"*Claro?*" Mojo said.

"*Si, Jefe,*" Luis replied. He opened the car door, felt the vacuum seal of air pressure change, and stepped outside. Shutting the door behind him, he touched the holstered weapon in the crook of his arm. under his windbreaker and walked toward the entrance of the pawnshop.

Pete and Daryl were in Pete's office. Daryl had filled him in on the details of his meeting with Ray. Even though Ray hadn't thought much of Pete's operation and Daryl's involvement, Pete still respected Ray. Pete had offered his condolences and was happy to hear Daryl and Ray were going to make amends. Daryl had also given Pete Ronald's envelope, and once Pete had made sure it was all there, Pete poured himself his end-of-the-evening drink. Since Daryl had mentioned Ray, Pete and Daryl began to discuss some of their favorite fights.

"Gropper," Pete suddenly said.

"What?" Daryl looked behind him to see the monitor above his shoulder. The display fed from a camera and covered the entirety of the counter out front. He saw Gropper standing in the middle of the frame.

"Shall we?" Pete stood up.

"Sure."

The two of them went through the office door and to the counter. Initially, the room had been part of a warehouse, and the counter connected to a mesh cage; Pete, however, had gotten rid of the cage years ago.

"I was hoping I could speak with Daryl for a moment," Gropper said when they entered the room.

Before anyone could say anything, the bell chimed, and the front door opened, and a thickset Latino with a beard walked in.

The man nodded to the three of them and practically did a doubletake when he saw Daryl. The Latino uttered something in Spanish and reached into his jacket.

Pete stepped in front of Daryl before the guy could get off a clear shot. The initial projectiles hit Pete in the sternum. He gasped and fell to the ground. Daryl caught one of the cartridges, hit the light switch, and dropped to the ground as Gropper hopped over the counter.

He heard the Latino continue to fire until he emp-tied the cylinder. In the darkness, Gropper felt around the shelf under the counter for anything he could use as a weapon. He didn't worry about making noise, as the gunman's hearing had probably been compromised. By now, Gropper's eyesight was used to the dimness and the subtle light from the inside office casting a hue on everything. He continued searching the shelf until he wrapped his fingers around what felt like the thick end of a pool cue.

He crouched so he could peer over the edge of the counter. The man was backlit through the door. He had reloaded and was moving the weapon slowly from side to side. Too many video games.

Gropper waited until the man pointed away the weapon, stood, and ran around the edge of the counter toward his foe.

The pool cue had once been the prized possession of a hustler named Jenkins. The guy's nickname was one of the border states, but it had been forgotten over time. He had become delinquent paying off his losses and rather than have his fingers broken, he offered the only thing he thought worthwhile as collateral.

Normally, Pete wouldn't have accepted something with less intrinsic value than what he had been owed, but he saw how much Jenkins had worshipped the cue, so he took it. Jenkins had died of a heart attack before he could get his cue out of hock and, over time, the item collected dust. Pete had the thing appraised by a specialist, but ultimately collectors weren't that inter-ested. After a few years had gone by, Pete no longer kept it out for resale.

Gropper closed the distance. He swung one-handed, like he was hitting a forehand in tennis. He connected somewhere on the side of the man's skull. In the dark, it was difficult to tell the location, but the man's body crumpled. Enough light still shone from the front, so Gropper kicked the gun away, found the switch, and turned on the shop lights.

The man was on the ground, half-conscious. Blood was pooling on the floor, and the man pawed at the air with his left hand. Gropper calmly walked back over and finished what he had started. Then he went over-hand with the cue, like he was driving in a railroad spike. He delivered the coup de grâce and went to check on Pete and Daryl.

Mojo heard the gunshots—two by themselves and then four more in quick succession. Based on the second grouping, Mojo could only assume Luis had fired the weapon.

He had not considered a contingency plan should there be gunfire, but already his mind was racing, ex-amining possible options. The first: Luis had been overzealous and an opportunity to take out Gropper had presented itself. While this was not outside of the realm of possibilities, Mojo didn't think Luis would have made that decision. Sure, the kid was still green, but he didn't seem undisciplined.

The second and more likely: Luis had been made by Gropper and defended himself. It certainly wouldn't be the first time a savvy veteran had been bested by a new-comer. Mojo remembered listening to his father talking about football matches in which teams who were heavily favored had been beaten by much less talented opponents.

"It's why they play the games," Mojo said aloud, echoing the phrase his father had often repeated. It had only been a single weapon that had fired. So, if Luis had in fact killed Gropper, then he would be returning to the car soon.

Of course, there also could have been a third, unexplainable reason that involved factors outside of Mojo's knowledge. This was the most likely option. So, he would wait another thirty seconds for Luis. If he didn't return, it was safe to assume he's been killed. Mojo had done enough reconnaissance; he would regroup and return for Gropper once the dust settled again.

Mojo waited another twenty seconds and when Luis didn't emerge from the shop, pulled the car out of the spot, and headed back to the motel.

Daryl was still pretty lucid, considering the amount of blood he'd lost, but he was also in a lot of pain. Gropper tried to be as gentle as he could but administering first aid hadn't been his specialty.

Daryl's shirt had soaked though, but it looked like the bleeding had stopped for now. Gropper helped Daryl to his feet, guided him past the dead body, and out the front door.

He took the keys from Daryl, opened the passenger door of Daryl's car, and deposited the injured man on the seat. Quickly, Gropper returned to the pawnshop. Once inside, he placed the pool cue handle in Pete's hand. It wouldn't fool any crime scene technicians, but he figured they might not try so hard to connect the dots if the murder weapon was found, and the Latino had priors.

Gropper slid into the driver's seat. "Which hospital?"

"No," Daryl answered. "I know a place we can go."

———

Daryl gave Gropper the address, took out his cell phone, and called 911. The pawnshop was legitimate; they were able to operate as payday advance lenders, which was also legal. Daryl would say it was a hold-up attempt gone wrong. He prepared the monologue he would give as he dialed the number. He felt light-headed, but still capable.

The dispatcher came on the line. Daryl said the name of the pawnshop and that he'd heard gunshots. The dispatcher began to ask more questions, but the phone slipped from Daryl's hand, and he passed out.

———

Gropper took Daryl to the house of a medical student from MUSC. The guy's name was Tyler. The man wore a blue t-shirt depicting the evolution of bicycles since their invention. He looked more like someone who had just checked into a hostel rather than a medical student.

Tyler also looked like he'd hadn't gotten a full night's sleep in a long time, but as soon as Gropper had mentioned Daryl and his condition, the man sprang into action. Gropper helped Tyler carry Daryl into the house, and they put him in a bathtub. Tyler did a very quick examination, but Daryl needed immediate medical attention, more than Tyler could give him.

Tyler said he would call for an ambulance and get Daryl to the hospital. Aside from tending to the wound and blood loss, they would need to do a CT scan to reveal if any of his internal organs had been damaged. The young man went to the living room, picked up the phone, and made the call.

Gropper stood in the living room and took in the place. The house was nice with artwork on the walls and a poster for a band called *Dread Medicine*. When he'd finished on the phone, Tyler saw Gropper checking out the poster.

"My brother Leonard's band," Tyler told him. "The ambulance should be here soon."

Gropper thanked Tyler for his help, said he would leave before the ambulance got there, but he would check on Daryl within the next few days. He asked Tyler for a change of shirt, and Tyler gave him a Dread Medicine t-shirt.

Outside, Gropper got into Daryl's car. He could have probably taken the steps to sanitize the car, but at this point, he figured the best thing would be to junk it. Depending on whether the police accepted the attempted robbery as the turn of events, Daryl might be able to claim his car had been stolen. Insurance may or may not cover it, but that wasn't Gropper's concern.

He found his favorite radio station, caught the middle of a segment on Dexter Gordon, and drove to a salvage yard. The owner had previously done business with McGill, so Gropper knew he wouldn't have a problem destroying the car.

Mojo passed the ball to his son Osvaldo, who had already been exhibiting exemplary skills for his age group. He watched Osvaldo take the pass, dribble, and shoot. Even though there was no goalie, it was still an impressive strike.

"*Buen trabajo,*" Mojo said.

"*Gracias.*" Osvaldo moved over to a set of cones and dribbled in a figure-eight pattern. In a few years, he would have the opportunity to play for an advanced age group, or so his current coach thought, *if* Osvaldo continued to develop at this rate.

Mojo was proud of his son and watched him almost effortlessly maneuver through the obstacles. He only regretted that Osvaldo's grandfather wasn't there. Mojo had never taken to the sport, and though Mojo's father had never mentioned it, he knew deep down the man had been disappointed. While they had some memorable times watching games on television, it wasn't the same.

"*Uno mas,*" Mojo said, then indicated they would have to head home so he could prepare dinner.

Osvaldo nodded and began another rotation. Yet another thing people wouldn't believe: Mojo was an excellent chef. While he'd never trained or attended a culinary school, he'd picked up enough through the years, and he enjoyed cooking for his family. His wife, Carmen loved to bake, so she was in charge of desserts.

It was a worthwhile trade-off.

Mojo had decided to head home the following day after visiting the pawnshop. He'd learned enough about Gropper to be able to return and pick up where he'd left off. With a police investigation into the pawnshop, he didn't want to risk anything. He'd reported what he'd found out, told the bosses about the situation with Luis, and said he would return in a few weeks or if the investigation settled, whichever happened first. He was given a retainer and told they would take him up on his offer.

Osvaldo retrieved the ball from the net. Mojo collected the cones from the ground and thought about the marinade he would use on the pork shoulder when they got home.

Gropper found Tyler getting coffee in the hospital's cafeteria. Though Tyler still looked sleep-deprived, Gropper realized this was probably the typical look of a med student. They sat at a table and Tyler was able to provide the details of Daryl's prognosis.

Daryl had gone into surgery almost immediately. The puncture wound had been dealt with; however, his lower intestine had been perforated. It appeared he would be in the clear, but they would need to monitor him closely for the next few weeks.

"The cops showed up to ask him some questions." Tyler took a sip of coffee and suddenly waved his hand back and forth to suggest it wasn't a big deal. "He wasn't able to tell them anything, though."

Whether it was actually the case or not, Daryl claimed to have no memory of the incident. The trauma he'd suffered, and the amount of painkillers he'd taken, meant without a witness there was no way to get an accurate version of the events. Gropper nodded. He would ask McGill to check with any of his former colleagues to see what, if any, progress the police had made. He thanked Tyler again, told him he'd cleaned the shirt, and Tyler could have it back if he wanted it.

"You keep it," Tyler said. "I've got plenty of them."

McGill took a bite of sausage and chased it with coffee. As soon as his cup hit the table, Sue stepped over with the pot to give him a refill. The scene reminded McGill of a meeting he'd had with a confidential informant, JP, years ago, when McGill was still on the force.

JP had liked to frequent the same bar. He told

McGill when he would walk through the threshold, the bartender would change songs on the stereo to "Fountain and Fairfax" by the Afghan Whigs and immediately begin fixing JP a "Blacktooth Grin."

"It's nice to have a place like that," JP had said.

"Afghan Whigs?"

So began an hour-long recitation of the Afghan Whigs catalog and history. McGill would learn very quickly to be more careful with his questions in future.

McGill took another sip of coffee and smiled at the memory. Gropper appeared at the entrance, made his way over to the table, and sat down. He unzipped his jacket and revealed a purple t-shirt with "Dread Medicine" above what looked like a skull and crossbones made of electric guitars.

"Formal attire?" McGill smirked.

Gropper caught up McGill on the new developments, including how Daryl was adjusting at the hospital, and asked if McGill would look into how the investigation was progressing. McGill assured Gropper he would.

"The band's not bad either." Gropper indicated the shirt. The waiter brought him a green tea.

Both men took some time drinking their respective drinks before Gropper spoke again. "Sheldon and Ivan?"

McGill offered that he'd reached out to Ivan and suggested they wouldn't have to worry about settling the loan. He didn't think there would be forgiveness in paying anything back, but he doubted the operation would be up and running again anytime soon. Pete's funeral was scheduled to take place in a few weeks, just about the time Daryl was going to be discharged from the hospital. Both Gropper and McGill were going to attend.

"How's Art Hare settling into the new place?" McGill asked.

"Well."

Mr. Hare's needs could no longer be addressed exclusively by Hare's son, so McGill had recommended an assisted living facility that housed a former client of McGill's from when he first started his business. Gropper had helped Mr. Hare move into his new place and while Art Hare could no longer join Gropper and McGill when they conducted business, Gropper promised he would keep Mr. Hare in the loop with the goings on at the diner.

"And so, we ask you to accept ..." the priest said and continued with the service.

There were about ten people in the church. Gropper assumed most were probably extended family. McGill left when the proceedings concluded. It had been one of the few times he had seen him outside of the diner in the last couple of years.

Gropper got into a line of people sharing their condolences with Daryl. While Daryl had recovered well, considering what had happened, he still had a long way to go. He'd recently traded in the wheelchair for a cane.

Tyler, who had been in the line ahead of Gropper, noticed him and turned around. "Hey. Hope you're well."

"Thanks," Gropper said. "You, too."

"This is my brother, Leonard," Tyler said, and Leonard and Gropper shook hands. "Nice to meet you."

"Likewise." Leonard's cell phone rang. "Sorry," he said and took a few steps away. He looked at incoming call and his brow furrowed. "Hello. Of course, I'll be right there." He hung up the phone and quickly returned to Tyler and Gropper. "I gotta go. That was Mon. She's ready; I told her I'd take her today."

"Go," Tyler told him. "I'll take care of everything."

Leonard said goodbye to Gropper, excused himself, said a quick word to Daryl, and left. Tyler went on to tell Gropper that Leonard and his bandmates had been trying to get Monica, another musician, into rehab.

"It's been difficult to get her to go get treatment, so ..."

"I understand," Gropper said with a nod.

Both men continued walking toward the exit where Daryl was. Tyler offered his condolences, said goodbye to Gropper as well, and continued into the parking lot.

"Wait for me," Daryl called to Gropper. "I'll give you a ride."

"OK," Gropper exited the church. He had driven, but he could leave his car and retrieve it later. He continued through the parking lot. The cemetery was on the other side, so he took the time to go visit Ms. Bradley's final resting place.

Gropper had been uncertain as to his next move now that staying with the Hares was off the table, but if they would have him back, he'd ask Liz and Connie if he could stay with them.

While returning to them would violate one of his rules, he also realized he needed to adapt. He left another rock on Ms. Bradley's headstone and continued to ruminate upon the situation. He could make it work.

Gropper returned to the church parking lot. Daryl was finishing up with the last person.

"Come on," Daryl said and motioned Gropper to follow him. "I'm over here."

The two men walked to a Honda Accord.

"Insurance came through," Daryl said and gestured toward the car.

Both men got inside.

"Thank you." Daryl started the engine.

"No problem," Gropper said.

"Where am I taking you?"

"The diner."

"Cool, I just need to make a stop first."

Daryl pulled up the car outside of Floyd's gym. "Be right back."

He took the cane from the back seat and ambled to the front door. It opened and a large man with a cast stood in the entry way, next to a shepherd of some kind. The dog's tail wagged when Daryl approached. The dog came over and while it was difficult for him to maneuver, he bent down and pet the dog.

He spoke to the man in the cast, though Gropper couldn't hear what they said. The man picked up a trophy from the floor, shut the door with the dog inside, and followed Daryl back out to the car. He opened the back seat, placed the trophy inside, and shut the door.

"This is Ronald," Daryl told Gropper.

"Nice to meet you," Ronald said.

Daryl rolled down the driver's side window and Ronald leaned in so they could speak.

"How much time again on the Stairmaster?" Ronald asked.

"Half an hour," Darryl answered and turned the key in the ignition. "Then ten minutes of stretching, and we do some HIIT training."

"HIIT?"

"High-intensity intervals."

Ronald exhaled noisily and his shoulders sank.

"We're going to whip you into shape," Daryl said confidently.

"OK." Ronald tapped the hood and walked back to the gym.

Daryl pulled out of the spot and continued to drive toward the diner.

"How much longer do you rehab?" Gropper asked.

"Physical therapy's another two weeks, then we'll see." Daryl didn't have his full range of motion yet, but he was making progress. He went on to say that he was going to take over running the gym, teach some classes, maybe train some fighters.

"Who knows?" Daryl added with a shrug. There was a buyer interested in the pawnshop. "Not the place itself, but the land."

It was too good of an offer for Daryl to pass up. Pete hadn't had any children, so the shop had gone to Daryl. He had offered Pete's ex-wife some of the proceeds, so she wouldn't hinder the sale.

They pulled into the diner's parking lot.

"Thank McGill for me," Daryl said.

"I will." Gropper looked at the trophy in the back seat. "Where to next?"

"Friend of mine's just had surgery. They said to bring something that might raise his spirits. This was the first thing we won together."

"Gotcha, well,"—Gropper opened the door—"see you around."

"Yeah, swing by the gym."

"Will do."

Gropper shut the door and Daryl pulled away. He walked inside the diner and took a seat at the table. McGill was dowsing fries in ketchup and mayonnaise.

Even though he'd only moved in a few weeks ago, and hadn't lived with them in a long time, it felt like

Gropper had never left. Connie still favored the same routine as he had remembered: drinks with colleagues, or a night in with a glass of wine and sweats. Liz, however, had changed pretty radically.

Gone was the little girl who was enamored with playing hide-and-seek and kept tabs on Gropper. While Liz was still a charming and well-behaved kid, she had grown up. During the first few days, Gropper processed nostalgia, and adapted to the new situation. He would happily return to spending time with Connie as she decompressed from work. Liz spent the majority of her time outside the house. Every so often, the three of them would have dinner, but those moments were rare.

That morning, after Connie left to begin a new shift, and Liz was picked up for school, Gropper began his day. First, he'd pick up Daryl at the gym and they would go to the cemetery so they could both pay their respects to Pete and Ms. Bradley. Daryl also wanted to see if Gropper would be interested in teaching a jiu-jitsu class. Rather than discuss it on the phone, Daryl suggested they talk about it on the way.

Daryl was waiting outside the gym with the shepherd when Gropper pulled up.

"Hey, Ronald asked if I could watch Ajax for the day. Cool if he comes with us?"

"Not a problem." Gropper pushed open the passenger door, slid the seat forward, and Ajax dutifully hopped in and curled up in the back.

"Thanks." Daryl got in and closed the door.

Ajax leaned forward and licked Daryl's hand.

"It's funny," Daryl began and indicated the dog. "He and I didn't always get along."

Gropper turned down the volume on the radio, and they pulled out. Daryl had opted for more of a soft-sell approach to teaching. He suggested teaching a class and training some pupils had given him a new lease on life.

It had also certainly helped with his recovery. Though it was not something Gropper had actually considered, he knew McGill and his business would have to end at some point. What would Gropper do then? Teaching a class at the gym might not be a bad option.

"Let me think about it," Gropper said.

"Take your time." Gropper pulled into the parking lot by the cemetery. "I'm going to let him go to the bathroom. I'll meet you in there." Daryl exited the car and took the dog with him.

Gropper watched them disappear, then turned and headed into the cemetery. At this time of day, there weren't very many other people there. In fact, there was only one other car in the parking lot: a beat-up Hyundai.

Gropper walked to Ms. Bradley's grave and cleaned some of the fallen leaves from the marker. He didn't leave a rock this time but took some liner notes from a Bill Evans CD he'd found when he'd packed up his room and laid them down by the stone.

He heard Ajax bark, turned, and saw the dog escape from Daryl. Ajax sprinted toward Gropper with his teeth bared.

Mojo didn't have an ethical code, but if he could avoid unnecessary unpleasantness, then he would. On the opposite end of the spectrum from those who were insane were those who were inflexible moralists. They had rules they would never break. Mojo was somewhere closer to that end, but he was further toward the middle. If Mojo had the opportunity to take out a target, but it meant there might be some collateral damage, then so be it. Of course, if he would always take an alternative, if it were possible.

Therefore, he decided he wouldn't engage with Gropper when the man was at home with the woman or her daughter. Instead, Mojo chose to wait for Gropper to go to the cemetery.

Mojo had gotten there ahead of time, parked, and sat underneath a tree. He had bought a paperback with him. It was a nice day, so it turned out to be quite pleasant. Eventually, the man Gropper showed up at the cemetery. He waited a moment for Gropper to relax, then he removed a silenced Sig Sauer P226.

Mojo heard the dog bark, looked over, and saw the animal break free from its owner. The dog was heading straight at him. Mojo aimed. The stone clipped him on the shoulder, and Mojo fired low.

He tried to pull the trigger again, but the dog was already on him. The animal bit down on Mojo's calf. He yelled in pain. He was about to get another shot off when his world went black.

Gropper watched Ajax approach and saw the animal looking past Gropper. As he turned, he noticed the man.

The dog raced by Gropper as the man raised a silenced weapon, and Gropper's mind raced as to the professional's identity. He picked up a rock from the ground and hurled it. The rock made impact with the man's shoulder just as he squeezed off a round. Thankfully, it missed the canine.

Gropper was already in motion as the dog sank his teeth into the man's leg. The man yelled as Gropper approached … and connected with a roundhouse kick.

Daryl called off Ajax and told him to heel, and he did so. While Daryl had continued to make progress with his recovery, he still moved slowly. His footfalls were heavy as he got closer.

"Jesus," Daryl murmured. "Who is he?"

"I don't know." Gropper looked around. Though his emotions were rarely transparent, he was obviously concerned. He continued to scan the area.

"Get out of here," Daryl said. "I've got this."

"You sure?"

"Go!"

"Thank you." Gropper started toward his car while Daryl took out his phone to call the police.

—————

"You thought about the future at all?" Gropper asked as he sipped his tea.

McGill had just taken a bite of his pancake. He chewed and swallowed. Gropper had been at the diner for about a half an hour, and already McGill had gone through two entrees. The server who waited on them was new; a film buff who asked McGill if he'd ever seen the movie *Diner*, in which a character was going to attempt to eat all the meals from the left side of the menu.

"You mean, after this?" McGill indicated the plate in front of him, then assured Gropper he knew what he had meant. "A little," McGill began and shrugged. "Not really, though. You?"

"More so lately," Gropper said.

He had debated moving out of Liz and Connie's place and finding a new place. Even after McGill had told Gropper about Mojo's resume, and the man's expertise, Gropper was still uneasy the guy had gotten the drop on him. Mojo had had an open file with almost every law enforcement acronym around the world. When the local police apprehended him and ran his prints, the computer lit up like a slot machine that had just hit a jackpot. Representatives from the State department flew in to oversee the proceedings and manage the extradition which would have to take place.

In the meantime, Mojo was transferred to a more secure offsite facility. None of this lessened Gropper's sense of dread. Had Ajax not been there … Gropper tried not to think about it, but it was difficult. However, ultimately, he realized his need to be with Liz and Connie outweighed his concern. As much as he wanted to prevent anything from happening to them, he also knew he needed them in his life. So, he decided to stay at their house. He could always reconsider his decision at a later date.

"I'm happy to discuss things," McGill said. "Let me get some French toast first."

"I'm not ready to hang it up yet," Gropper confessed.

ABOUT THE AUTHOR

Andrew Davie has worked in theater, finance, and education. He taught English in Macau on a Fulbright Grant and has survived a ruptured brain aneurysm and subarachnoid hemorrhage. He has published short stories at various places, books with All Due Respect, Next Chapter, Close to the Bone, Alien Buddha Press, and a memoir.

To learn more about Andrew Davie and discover more Next Chapter authors, visit our website at www.nextchapter.pub.

The Vig
ISBN: 978-4-82416-110-9
Mass Market

Published by
Next Chapter
2-5-6 SANNO
SANNO BRIDGE
143-0023 Ota-Ku, Tokyo
+818035793528

13th December 2022

www.ingramcontent.com/pod-product-compliance
Lightning Source LLC
LaVergne TN
LVHW031240190726
843491LV00012B/3067